Cat's Witch
and the
Lost Birthday

TIGER series

Damon Burnard	*Revenge of the Killer Vegetables*
Lindsay Camp	*Cabbages from Outer Space*
Mick Fitzmaurice	*Morris Macmillipede*
Elizabeth Hawkins	*Henry's Most Unusual Birthday*
Kara May	*Cat's Witch*
	Cat's Witch and the Lost Birthday
	Cat's Witch and the Monster
	Cat's Witch and the Wizard
	Tracey-Ann and the Buffalo
Barbara Mitchelhill	*The Great Blackpool Sneezing Attack*
Penny Speller	*I Want to be on TV*
Robert Swindells	*Rolf and Rosie*
John Talbot	*Stanley Makes It Big*
Joan Tate	*Dad's Camel*
Hazel Townson	*Amos Shrike, the School Ghost*
	Blue Magic
	Snakes Alive!
	Through the Witch's Window
Jean Wills	*Lily and Lorna*
	The Pop Concert
	The Salt and Pepper Boys

KARA MAY

Cat's Witch
and the
Lost Birthday

Illustrated by Doffy Weir

Andersen Press·London

Text © 1994 by Kara May
Illustrations © 1994 by Doffy Weir

First published in 1994
by Andersen Press Limited,
20 Vauxhall Bridge Road, London SW1V 2SA.
This edition published 2002.

British Library Cataloguing in Publication Data available
ISBN 0 86264 532 8

Phototypeset by Intype, London
Printed and bound in China

1

Cat and his witch, whose name was Aggie, lived in a house with a hole in the roof.

Cat peered down it.

In the room below, Aggie was reading the *Witchety News*. Dirty cups and other mess lay all around her.

'You said you'd tidy up while I swept the roof,' bristled Cat.

'I didn't say when!' chuckled Aggie.

'Never mind that now.' Cat leapt down beside her. 'I've been thinking about the roof hole. It looks as if we can't be bothered to mend it. That's what people will think!'

Aggie gave a toothy grin. 'They can think what they like. A roof hole is just what I need to come and go on my broomstick.'

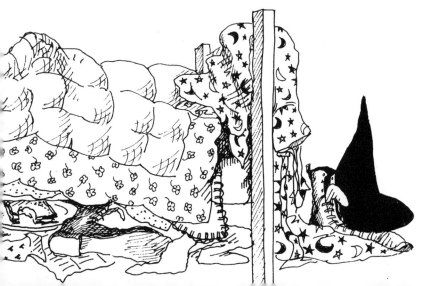

Cat opened his mouth to say, 'Why not use the door?' when there was a knock on it. They went to see who it was.

It was little Ali Shah.

'I've got something for you,' he said.

Ali held out an envelope. In it was an invitation to Wantwich's fiftieth birthday. 'I'm helping the postman to give them out,' he said proudly.

Aggie's face clouded over.

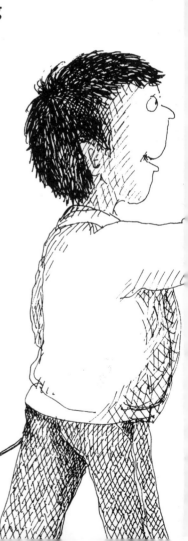

'All this fuss, fuss, fuss over the town's birthday! Even the ducks in the park are quacking about it.'

'But it's exciting,' said Ali. 'The French are coming from Lilleville, our twin town in France. The Mayor just told me.'

Aggie shrugged. 'The French

9

and the whole universe can come
for all I care. I'm not going.'

'She never goes to birthday
parties,' said Cat. 'But I shall
come. The French are my sort of
people.' He smoothed his
whiskers. 'They have charm and
good food and fine manners
and style.'

'Aggie, please come too,' said
little Ali Shah.

Aggie shook her head so hard

her hair whirled round. 'I don't like birthdays.'

Ali's eyes widened. 'Not even your own?'

Aggie sighed. 'I haven't had a birthday for hundreds of years. I don't know when it is. I must have known once, but somehow or other I've lost the date.'

Ali was all concern. 'That's awful! Haven't you got a spell to find it in your *Super Witch Spellbook*?'

'I've looked, but there isn't one,' said Aggie. Tears watered her eyes and Cat gave a weary sigh.

'Talk of birthdays always does this to her. Except for peeling onions, it's the only thing that makes her cry. You'd better go, Ali. She can carry on like this for hours.'

Aggie sat with the tears streaming down. She didn't know herself why her lost birthday upset her so much. It was a mystery she'd never been able to understand. 'No one else's birthday is a mystery! Why should

mine be?' she sobbed. 'It's not
fair!'

She went on and on, weeping
and wailing. Cat was thinking he
couldn't stand it much longer
when a face
peered in at
the window.
It was the
Mayor of
Wantwich.

'I knocked but no one heard,' she said.

Aggie's tears suddenly stopped. 'Tell her to clear off, Cat. I'm not in the mood to look at her, never mind talk to her.'

'Oh yes you are,' said Cat. The Mayor didn't like Aggie anymore than Aggie liked her. 'She wouldn't be here unless she wanted something.' Cat went on, 'That something must be paid for, and we need the money.'

He greeted the Mayor with a smile and a bow. The Mayor's face was pink with pleasure as she followed him in. But Aggie gave her a stony stare.

'So, the Melon's come to call! This *is* an honour,' she said, as if it was an honour she could do without. The Mayor's face turned from pink to purple.

'I have told you before, Aggie, I am not the Melon of Wantwich, but the Mayor.'

Aggie grinned. 'And I keep forgetting. Silly me. I keep getting mixed up because –'

Cat knew the 'because'. It was because the Mayor was large and round. 'Let's get down to business,' he put in quickly. 'We all know the Mayor is a busy woman.'

'Thank you, Cat. It's a pleasure to do business with you,' smarmed the Mayor, with a sneer down her nose at Aggie.

'Hmph!' snorted Aggie, and raised her foot. Cat thought she was going to boot the Mayor out.

'Aggie, don't!' he hissed.

But Aggie's foot went for a cushion.

WHAM!

It went flying up through the
hole in the roof. Then back!
'Ouch!' cried the Mayor, as it
landed THUMP! on her head.

Aggie turned on the cushion
and waved her wand.

'Say "Sorry" to the Melon, I mean, Mayor,' she commanded.

At once a face looked out of the cushion.

'Sorry,' it said, and vanished.

The Mayor sighed. 'Whatever you are or aren't you are a magical witch, Aggie. That is why I am here. It's about the town's fiftieth birthday –'

Before the Mayor could go on, Aggie covered her ears.

'Don't say that word in my house!' she screeched.

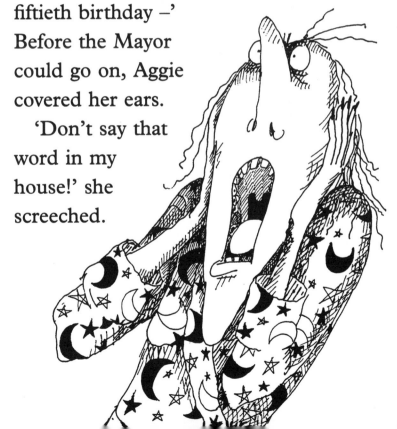

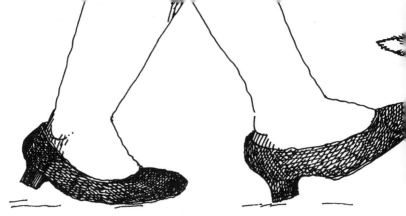

'You can say it to me,' said Cat, taking the Mayor outside.

Quickly the Mayor explained she'd had a phone call from the Mayor of Lilleville.

'*Monsieur le Maire*, which is French for Mr Mayor, said someone in Lilleville had heard about Aggie from a friend of a friend of a friend. They'd asked him to ask me if she'd do magic at our party. And I said, "Yes." '

Cat raised an eyebrow.

'Without having asked Aggie?'

The Mayor nodded. 'I felt I had to say "yes" or the French wouldn't come, and the town would be so disappointed. Aggie can name her own price,' she added.

Cat's eyes gleamed. 'Leave it to me. Come back later.'

He went to report to Aggie.

'Don't bother,' she said. 'I heard what the Melon said. The answer's "no". I'm on strike.'

'On strike!' blustered Cat.

'Other people have birthdays. Other people go on strike. I'm going to strike till my lost birthday is found.'

Cat shook the all but empty money-box. 'What about the name-your-own-price money?'

'Strikers have to suffer for what they want, and what I want is my birthday.'

'And what about our French guests?' Cat demanded. 'They have done you the honour of asking to see your magic. It would be rude to refuse. And you know what I feel about manners.'

Aggie groaned. 'Don't I just! You care more about manners than me! It's nothing to you I've been birthdayless for hundreds of years.'

She began to weep and wail.

'Don't start that again!' said
Cat.

But Aggie wailed on, 'I wish I
had a birthday. I wish, I wish
I did!'

'I've had enough for one day.
Stop that racket. Please!' said
Cat.

Aggie opened her mouth. Out
came her loudest wail yet. Cat's
red eyes glowed, which meant he
was very angry.

'I warn you,
Aggie, if you
don't stop,
I'm off!'

Now it was

Aggie's eyes that glowed.

'You are my cat. You wouldn't dare leave me!'

As soon as the words were out of her mouth, Aggie wished she could put them back in. A dare was something Cat could never resist.

25

Cat froze where he stood.

Then, without a word, he strode out of the door.

Aggie was so taken aback, it was some time later she ran to the window. But there was no sign of Cat.

One large tear rolled down her nose.

'I've lost my birthday. And I've lost my cat too,' said Cat's witch Aggie.

2

Aggie sat in her chair. For one full hour, dark angry clouds passed over her face.

'How could he leave me!' she raged. 'Cats don't leave their witches. It's not done!'

But as the first minute of the new hour struck, Aggie's anger turned on herself. It was she who'd dared Cat to leave her.

'He is my cat. This is his home! And I've driven him out! Oh, Cat, Cat, Cat! What will become of you!?'

At just that moment, Cat was asking himself the same question. It was all very well walking out on Aggie but soon it would be teatime, his tummy would need food. Then, he'd need a bed to sleep in.

He was wondering what to do when his nose twitched. There

was just one thing that made it twitch like that. Fish! He looked round to see Mr Snailey, the postman, on his way home from work. Under his arm was a large paper-wrapped parcel.

Cat's nose twitched again.

'Fish?' he asked.

Mr Snailey nodded.

'May I look?'

Without waiting for an answer, Cat took the parcel and unwrapped it.

'Trout, I thought so,' he said. Aggie never gave him fresh fish, or hardly ever. She couldn't be bothered to cook it. 'This will go down a treat for my tea. I've good news for you, Mr Snailey. I've left my witch and I'm going to live with you.'

Mr Snailey shook like an agitated jelly. He'd always been frightened of Aggie. What would she do if Cat left her for him? 'She might turn me into a frog or a mouse or, worse, a spider! I want

to stay a postman,' he quivered.

But Cat held the fish firmly
with one front paw, held Mr
Snailey's arm with the other, and
marched him off to No 23
Blossom Avenue, where Mr
Snailey lived. The house was
dust-free and tidy.

This is my sort of house,' said Cat. He took another sniff at the trout.

'We'll have it grilled, shall we?'
Mr Snailey liked his fish poached, but was too scared to

say, so Cat had the trout to himself. When he'd finished, Mr Snailey set about the washing-up.

'Aggie always left it to me or left it in the sink,' said Cat.

Mr Snailey shuddered. 'I like a clean sink,' he said. He took a duster and tin of polish from the cupboard. 'I must give the house a clean. I always do it after tea. Then I look at my stamp collection till bedtime.'

Cat started. 'But you're a postman! You're looking at stamps all day.'

'Yes, I know.' For the first time that evening, Mr Snailey smiled. 'I like stamps.'

Cat thought of his evenings
with Aggie. They might go for a
fly on the broomstick or make
a spell or roast marshmallows in
the fireplace.

'I suppose I could try looking
at stamps,' he said.

Mr Snailey had just opened his
stamp book when there was a
knock on the door. It was Ali
Shah. He'd come to say he'd
delivered the invitations. He was
surprised to see Cat.

'I didn't know you and Mr Snailey were friends. Is Aggie here too?' he asked.

'I've left Aggie,' said Cat.

Ali's mouth dropped. 'But she's your witch.'

The truth in Ali's words made Cat shiver. 'I had to leave,' he said, and went on to explain why.

'If I'd lost my birthday, I might go on strike. I don't blame Aggie for that. But I'm sad about the French not coming,' said Ali.

'I've learnt to say *bonjour* which is French for hullo.'

Cat paused. He felt uncomfortable inside. It was not a feeling he was used to.

'She dared me to leave, so I had to,' he said again.

'What if I dared you to go back?' asked Ali.

Cat laughed. 'Then I'd have to do it. You're a smart lad, Ali. But it'd make no difference to Aggie. I know my witch. Whether she wants to or not, she'll stay on strike till her birthday is found.'

'Please, may I speak?' said Mr Snailey.

That morning he'd had a letter for Wizard Wesley Wenzil who

used to live in Wantwich, and he'd sent it on to the Wizard's new address.

'If it hadn't been for the letter I wouldn't have thought of him but as it is, I have and please,' piped on Mr Snailey, 'I know the Wizard's not as magical as Aggie but he's got computers with lots of data on and he might have Aggie's birthday.'

Cat stared at Mr Snailey. 'I've never heard you say so many words at once.'

Mr Snailey went white, afraid he'd spoken out of turn and Cat would put a spell on him. But Ali was jumping up and down with excitement. 'It's a brilliant idea, Mr Snailey. Cat, please, go and tell Aggie.'

Cat looked round the dust-free sitting-room with the stamp collection neatly piled on the dust-free table. Then, there was

Mr Snailey himself who would cook him fish and do the cleaning. But Mr Snailey had no magic. 'I've only been here a few hours, and I'm bored,' thought Cat.

'Well?' asked Ali. 'Can I dare you to go back?'

Mr Snailey crossed his fingers and hoped.

'Yes,' said Cat.

'Then I dare you!' said Ali.

'I can never resist a dare,' grinned Cat. 'Thanks for the fish, Mr Snailey,' he said, remembering his manners. 'And thank you for the idea about the Wizard. It's a good one.'

Soon after, he was back at Roof Hole House. He looked in through the window. Aggie was pacing back and forth, the tears flooding fast.

'Oh, Cat, please come back! I'll give you fish once a week and take my turn at cleaning.'

'Done!' said Cat.

He leapt in beside her.

'In return,' he said, 'I'll help you to find your lost birthday.'

Aggie gave her toothy grin. 'I should think so indeed. You are my cat.'

Cat was about to tell her Mr Snailey's idea, when the Mayor arrived. She was in such a state that her words came in a rush.

'I've just heard you're on strike, Aggie,' she said. 'Your birthday must be a terrible loss, I quite see that. But if you won't do your magic, the French won't come and the town's birthday won't be a glorious event but a f.l.o.p., FLOP!'

The Mayor had no breath to keep herself standing and sank

down into a chair which set her
chins wobbling.

Aggie paused. 'You did say
name your own price?' she said
at last.

The Mayor nodded so hard that
all her chins wobbled again.

'I said I'm on strike till my
birthday is found and I can't
unsay it. *But,*' Aggie went on, 'not
for you, not for Wantwich, but

43

for Cat and his love of good
manners, so as not to be rude to
the French, I'll do my best not
to be on strike and to find my
lost birthday.'

'Oh Aggie, thank you, I'm most
humbly grateful,' said the Mayor.

'Humbly grateful! I like that,' grinned Aggie, as the Mayor went off. She gave a yawn. 'We can think about the birthday hunt tomorrow.' Aggie paused.

'Er, um, Cat,' she said, and broke off.

Cat knew what the 'Er, um' meant.

'I'm glad I'm home too,' he said.

Aggie gave her toothy grin. 'I should think so indeed! Now let's get to bed. I've a feeling in my bones it will be a long day tomorrow,' said Cat's witch Aggie.

3

The next morning Aggie sat with
her hat pulled down over her
face. A 'mmm' came floating up
from underneath the hat. Cat
knew what it meant. It meant

Aggie was thinking about Mr Snailey's idea, which he'd told her about over breakfast. But he also knew not to say so or she'd squash the idea forever.

He was picking up the newspapers scattered on the floor when Aggie suddenly looked out from under her hat.

'I was thinking we might call on Wesley Wenzil,' she said, as if the thought had just flown into her mind. 'He's always asking me to call, it will be rude if I don't.'

Cat had to try hard not to grin,
but he managed it. 'When were
you thinking of going?'

'No time like the present!'
Aggie whistled up her
broomstick. WHHT!

WHHT!

A few minutes later,
they were at Wizard
Wenzil's or Wesley

as he liked to be called. In his spare time he did magic on TV because he liked showing off and being a star. But mostly he was at home, working on magical experiments.

'But work can wait! I'm thrilled to see you, Aggie.'

Aggie smiled. 'I was going to beat about the bush but the fact is, Wesley, I want to ask you something.'

Wesley listened.

'I've got the birth dates of witches born this century on computer,' he said. 'But you were born centuries before.'

Aggie sighed. 'That's that then. I'll have to stay on strike, the French won't come to Wantwich and the party will be a FLOP like the Melon said.'

'Maybe not! Wait!'

Wesley rushed off and came back with a test tube with a mixture in it of golden brown, like tiger's eyes.

'I've just been working on it. It's a *Brain Scan* mixture. It scans the brain for whatever you want that is stored in it. Your birthday will be in there somewhere. It's just that you've forgotten it.'

Aggie grinned. 'You might look like a flashy TV star, Wesley. But you're a whizz of a wizard.'

Wesley's face turned suddenly serious. 'I have to warn you, the mixture has yet to be tested. It could, I fear, not only scan the brain but blow it up.'

Cat was on his feet at once. 'Forget it, Aggie. I'm not going to let you risk that.'

'Thank you, Cat,' said Aggie. But she took the mixture from Wesley. 'Now let's get back to Wantwich.'

As they flew down to Roof Hole House, they saw not only the Mayor, but all the town.

Ali rushed up. 'Are you still on strike, Aggie?'

Cat told them what had happened. The Wantwichers gave a horrified gasp. 'Don't take it, Aggie,' they said. 'We'd rather have a flop birthday than lose you.'

Aggie stared at them in astonishment. It was the first time the people of Wantwich had put her first. She turned to the Mayor. 'What do you say?'

'Aggie Witch, you and I don't get on and maybe we never will. But Wantwich wouldn't be Wantwich without you. It's not worth the risk of losing you.'

Aggie stared at the Mayor to see if she was joking.

But she saw the Mayor was not.

'Wait here,' said Aggie. 'I need to think.'

She went on into the house.

'Aggie, say "no". Please,' said Cat. 'What would I do without you?'

Aggie smiled at him. 'You could go and live with Mr Snailey. But the fact is,' she went on, 'I've been

55

looking for my birthday for all these years. Now is my chance to find it. I must ask myself if I should.'

She shut her eyes.

Cat held his breath.

'The answer is "yes"!' said Aggie.

At once she swallowed the mixture.

'Scan my brain for my lost birthday!' she said.

There was a sudden bright light.

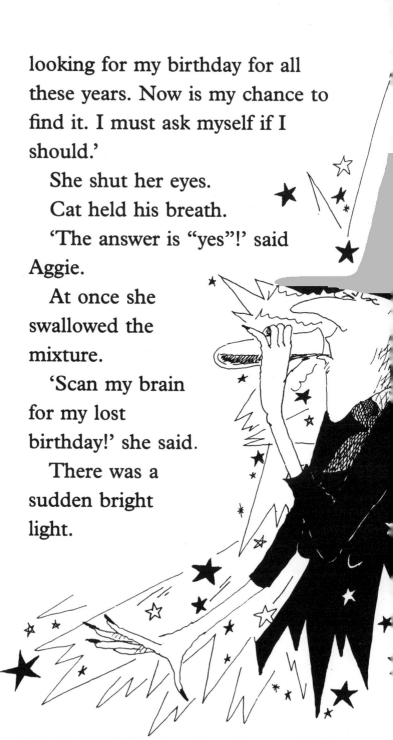

On the wall, as if on a screen, flashed the image of a little girl.

'That's me!' said Aggie.

Aggie and Cat watched to see what would happen next.

They saw Little Aggie run down the stairs.

Excitedly, she went into a large room.

She walked round the large table.

It was laden with birthday food and balloons hung from the ceiling and birthday crackers whizzed round the air.

Little Aggie clapped her hands. 'I can't wait for everyone to come. I've been waiting for my party for ages.'

She waited for the bell to ring.

But it didn't.

She had asked twenty-five children.

But not one of them came, not one.

'They've forgotten,' said Little Aggie.

She ran to her bedroom and took down the calendar with her birthday marked on it.

She tore out the day of her birthday and ripped it to shreds.

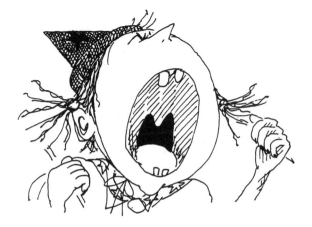

'I'll never have another
birthday. I hate birthdays. I don't
want another one ever!'

She jumped into her bed and
pulled the covers over her head.

Then the wall went blank.

'Oh,' said Aggie.

'Oh, Aggie,' said Cat.

Aggie sighed. 'I lost my
birthday on purpose.' Then she
realised she'd lost it again. 'I was
so upset I didn't look at the date
on the calendar.'

'It was 15th April, the same as Wantwich's birthday,' said Cat.

Aggie gave a smile so bright it put a shine all over her face. 'This is my town and I am its witch and we share our birthdays together. What a happy little witch, I am, I am.'

She ran outside to give the news.

61

'I'm alive and off strike and I've found my birthday. Wantwich shall have the most magical birthday ever!'

Aggie kept her word. She made a forest appear in the sky.

She made fountains of stars shoot up from the ground.

She made sunbeams dance on the table.

The Mayor of Lilleville kissed her hand. 'Your town is lucky to have you. If you ever want to move to France, we should be honoured. And Cat, of course, would be welcome.'

Ali ran up and tugged at her sleeve. 'You can't leave us, Aggie. Look what we've got for your birthday.'

63

The Mayor came forward with a cake ablaze with candles. Mr Snailey followed with his postman's sack bulging with cards and presents.

With one voice, everyone sang 'Happy Birthday' to Aggie. Then, she cut the cake and wished.

'What did you wish?' asked Cat, when at last they were home.

But she wasn't telling.

'But this I can tell you. Now my lost birthday is found, I shall never lose it again,' said Cat's witch Aggie.